SCARY
STORIES
FOR SLEEP-OVERS #8

By Craig Strickland

Illustrated by Dwight Been

LOWELL HOUSE JUVENILE

LOS ANGELES

For Ruthie, my best friend
—C.S.

To my brother and all my sisters
—D.B.

Library of Congress Catalog Card Number: 97-17225
ISBN: 1-56565-714-4

Publisher: Jack Artenstein
Editor in Chief, Roxbury Park Books: Michael Artenstein
Director of Publishing Services: Rena Copperman
Managing Editor: Lindsey Hay

Roxbury Park is an imprint of Lowell House,
A Division of the RGA Publishing Group, Inc.

Lowell House books can be purchased at special discounts when ordered in bulk for premiums and special sales.
Contact Department TC at the following address:

Lowell House
2020 Avenue of the Stars, Suite 300
Los Angeles, CA 90067

Manufactured in the United States of America
10 9 8 7 6 5 4 3 2 1

Based on a design by Michele Lanci-Altomare

Contents

Spiderbites

Something was wrong with Kativa's leg.

She felt it even before she opened her eyes that morning—a dry burning sensation at the bottom of her right calf, near her ankle. Her fingertips found a raised area, its diameter the size of a nickel. The middle of the huge bump stung as if it had been shot with a needle.

Frowning, she kicked the sheets off and sat up in bed. A wedge of morning sun spotlighted a large red welt on her leg. She stared at it for a few seconds, her heart pounding tightly in her chest, then she flung herself out of bed and hurried into the hall.

In the next room Kativa's six-year-old sister saw her rushing by. "What's the matter, Tiva?" she called out,

5

blinking her eyes sleepily. Natasha's dark hair stuck straight up from the pillow, making her look like an exotic bird.

"Something bit me last night!" Kativa cried as she raced down the hall toward their parents' room.

"Mom! Dad!" she yelled. "Look at my leg!"

Kativa's father rolled over, yawning. Her mother sat up in bed and stretched. "Calm down, honey," she said soothingly. "Come show me."

Kativa pulled up her pajama leg, revealing the red welt.

"Oh my," her mom gasped. Then her father sat up and squinted at Kativa's calf.

"I'll bet anything that's a spider bite," he said with another yawn.

"A *spider!*" Kativa cried, imagining the eight-legged creature still crawling around her room.

"I'll take care of it," her dad said, his head falling back down on the pillow. "Just as soon as I wake up."

···········

But it wasn't that easy.

Right after breakfast the entire family headed to Kativa's room. Kativa helped her mom change the sheets, then the two vacuumed the room. Her dad took up the carpet around the baseboards to see if there were any nests there. Then he brought a ladder into the room to check the molding near the ceiling for webs. Even Natasha did what she could, wriggling under the bed with a flashlight and timidly checking beneath the desk. But no one found anything.

"Thanks anyway," Kativa told her parents and sister.

"In a way, it's good we couldn't find it," her mom said. "That means whatever bit you is certainly not in this room now." And with that, her parents went out to clean up the breakfast dishes.

Kativa hung around her room for a while, pulling books off the shelf to look behind them. Then she put the pajamas she'd worn into the laundry bin. She wondered if something could have burrowed into her mattress, or if the tiny culprit had crawled into an electrical outlet. As Kativa rechecked every corner of her room, her sister, Natasha, sat on the edge of the bed, swinging her legs back and forth. Natasha liked to hang around her big sister and was always hoping that Kativa would have some time to play with her.

"Tiva, have you ever been bit by a spider before?" Natasha asked casually.

Kativa frowned, trying to remember. "I don't think so," she answered. "Why? Have you?"

Natasha stopped swinging her legs. Her eyes grew big and round as she considered the question. "Yes," she finally replied. "It was on our vacation last summer. It happened in that hotel we stayed in."

Kativa remembered seeing some tiny red marks on the back of her sister's hand. "But I thought Mom and Dad said those were *mosquito* bites," Kativa said with a frown.

Natasha shook her head firmly. "I know it was a spider. Of course, my bites weren't as big as yours," she explained. "I guess that's why Mom and Dad thought they were mosquito bites."

Kativa had a definite feeling her sister was making up this story to help her feel better. She decided to play along. "What was it like?" Kativa asked.

"I was scared at first, just like you," Natasha said breathlessly. "But later I decided it wasn't *that* bad being bitten by a spider."

"Thanks, Natasha," Kativa said with a smile. "I'll have to remember that."

....

That night Kativa wore clean pajamas and tucked herself between clean sheets. She had even changed her blanket and bedspread. The room had been searched by four people, and she had finally convinced herself it was completely spider-free.

But when she turned out the light, she began to picture something coming for her in the darkness. When she rolled over, a strand of her own hair brushed against her neck. She swatted at it, thinking something was scrambling along her skin. Every time the forced-air heater kicked on, bringing a loud blowing noise into the room, she jumped. Soon she was sure that from the dark ceiling above some unseen thing was lowering itself onto her from a slender thread.

Finally, Kativa turned on her light, climbed out of bed, and rummaged through her desk until she found the old seashell night-light she had used when she was Natasha's age. She plugged it into the outlet near her bed and smiled as the familiar pink-orange glow filled every dark corner of the room.

....

The next morning another big red welt appeared, this time on her left calf just below the knee.

Kativa shrieked in disbelief, then ran into her parents' room. "The spider got me again!" she screamed, pointing at her leg. "It's like it's . . . *hunting* me or something!"

Her parents came over, shaking their heads. Her mom washed the bite with alcohol, as she had done the morning before. And her dad knelt on one knee next to her, still knotting his tie. "I'm really sorry, honey," he said, his face grim as he studied the bite. "I'll call an exterminator to spray the entire house, inside and out. I promise you, there won't be an insect or a spider anywhere on our entire property!"

Kativa's eyes filled with tears. "I don't think I can stand to sleep in my room tonight," she moaned.

"I'll make up the bed in the guest room for tonight," her mom offered.

Kativa nodded, looking down at the matching bright red spider bites, one on each leg.

· · · · · · · · · · ·

When Kativa got home from school, the whole house smelled like bug spray, and she and her mom went around opening all the windows and setting up fans to blow some fresh air into the place. Kativa started to feel a little better after she spotted the bodies of tiny house spiders and moths lying on the floor, and she realized the exterminator's poison had done its job. Still, she refused to go anywhere near her own room.

Just before bedtime, Kativa finally asked Natasha to go in there to get her pajamas. She was sitting at the desk in the guest bedroom, making a halfhearted attempt to do some homework, when Natasha came in. "Here you go, Tiva," she said, setting down Kativa's pajamas and then lying down on the bed. "Whatcha doing?"

"I'm working on my endangered species report," Kativa said, thumbing through the papers before her. Normally, Kativa hated it when her sister bugged her while she was studying, but Natasha had been feeling sick all afternoon, and Kativa felt sorry for her. "You won't *believe* how much homework you're going to get, Natasha, when you're my—" She broke off her words, startled by her little sister's zombielike state.

Natasha wasn't listening. Instead, the little girl was staring down at the welts on Kativa's legs. "I know how you feel, you know," Natasha whispered dramatically. "The spider in that hotel bit *me* more than once, too."

"Really?" Kativa said in a weak voice.

"Yeah!" Natasha answered, her voice growing excited.

The truth of the matter was that the whole topic was starting to make Kativa feel very uncomfortable. She decided to change the subject. "Natasha, would you mind doing one more favor for me?" Kativa asked.

The little girl brightened. "Sure, Tiva! Anything!"

"Could you go into my room again and bring me my seashell night-light?"

Natasha, thrilled to have another mission, marched obediently down the hall.

···········

It was weird, sleeping in the guest room. Everything looked different. The Indian art prints on the wall, lit by the soft

11

reddish glow of her night-light, made it seem as if she were in some kind of museum. Even the noises of the house, like the distant hum of the refrigerator and the furnace, sounded different from this room.

She knew there couldn't possibly be any spiders here. There couldn't be any in her own room, either, or anywhere else in the whole house, thanks to the exterminator. Still, it took her a long time to fall asleep.

....

The bite was on her arm this time—on her left wrist, right where she would have worn a watch if she'd had one. Kativa didn't even scream when she awoke and saw it. She just felt weak. She lay in bed under the paintings of corn and handlooms and foxes and stared at her wrist as if she were trying to tell the time. *It's impossible,* she thought in confusion. *How did it find me in here?*

When her parents came in a few minutes later to wake her up for school, Kativa held up her arm without a word, tears glistening in her eyes. For a moment both grownups simply stared at the new red bump, their mouths open.

"I don't believe it!" her dad fumed. "That exterminator is coming right back here!"

"Let me try something first," her mom said, still examining Kativa's arm. "There's a man at the college who studies bugs. I think his name is Professor Weber. I've heard he knows everything about bugs, so maybe he can give us some advice."

Kativa's dad bent over her arm, shaking his head. "It's worth a try," he said. "Don't worry, Kativa. We'll find that spider."

....

Professor Weber's office, located in the biology building on the state college campus, was filled with bugs. Hundreds of butterflies, each pinned to a small mounting board, hung from the walls. The bookshelves were covered with volumes on insects. And in one corner of the room was a huge, glass-covered table housing the biggest assortment of spiders Kativa had ever seen. Everything from huge, hairy tarantulas to glossy black widows was under that glass, mounted and labeled.

"Quite a collection, don't you think?" said a tall man behind a desk in the corner. He stood up on lanky limbs and extended a long arm to Kativa's mother, his dark glassy eyes shining. "I'm Professor Weber." He grinned at Kativa. "And I understand you have a bug bite you want me to see."

Kativa nodded and pushed up her sleeve. "This is the third bite I've had," she began. "It happened just last—"

"Oh my," Professor Weber gasped. "That *is* a big one." He walked around his desk and over to Kativa and her mother with only two steps of his long, thin legs. Then he groped in his pockets and drew out a magnifying glass. "In fact, it's the biggest one I've ever seen."

"Is it . . . a spider bite?" Kativa asked in a quavering voice.

"Oh yes. Definitely. You can get some idea of the size of the spider that bit you by looking at the wound. See, there are two separate punctures. Those are fang marks."

Kativa stared down in horror at her arm. Now that the professor had mentioned it, she could make out two individual white spots, almost an inch apart. She cast a

13

glance at the nearly spider-filled table, her toes curling in her shoes. The spider that had made the marks on her arm was probably much bigger than any of the spiders in this room!

"What can we do about this, Professor Weber?" Kativa's mother asked. Her face was creased with worry. "This—this *thing* keeps biting my daughter every night!"

The tall man shrugged. "Some spiders actually show stalking behavior within their territories," he said. A little grin never quite left his face, as if he were amused by Kativa's situation. He turned toward her. "It appears that this spider has grown quite fond of you. Why don't you try moving to a different room?"

"I did!" Kativa cried out in frustration. "It got me there, too!"

"Oh my," the professor said. "That means your spider must have quite a large territory indeed." He fell silent and continued to look in fascination at Kativa's arm.

Her mom sighed impatiently. "Well?" she said. "Do you have *any* advice for us?"

Professor Weber sat down once more and put his elbows on the desk, placing the tips of his long fingers together. "Well, there is an old legend that comes to mind. It says that if a particular spider bites you four times, you will *turn into* a spider yourself," he said with a chuckle. "Didn't you say you'd been bitten three times now? That means maybe the next time—"

Kativa's mother suddenly rose to her feet. "What nonsense!" she spat. "My daughter is upset enough about these bites, Professor Weber. What business do you have trying to frighten her with silly stories like that!"

The tall man laughed. "Sorry. I don't believe that old myth, either, of course," he said, a tight little smile still on his face. "I was only trying to lighten you two up a little."

Kativa's mom rolled her eyes at her daughter. "Could you at least tell us what kind of spider this is, Professor Weber, so we know if it's dangerous?"

His face assumed a look of curiosity. "To tell you the truth, I have absolutely no idea. But I'd like to find out." His hands went together under his chin, making him look like a praying mantis. "There are still lots of secrets mankind hasn't found out about the spider world . . ."

Kativa's mom guided her toward the door. "Thank you, Professor Weber," she said curtly. "We'll figure something out."

"Say, if you catch the big pest, I'd really appreciate it if you'd bring it by!" the man called after them. "I'd love to do research on it."

Kativa turned around to cast one more glance at the insectlike professor. She was never happier to see a door slam on anyone in her life.

. . . .

At home, Kativa fell onto her parents' bed, exhausted. Her mom felt her head. "I think you have a fever, honey," she said. "Probably a reaction to the spider bites. It would probably do you good to try to take an afternoon nap."

"But, Mom!" Kativa said, looking around the room fearfully. "I'll just get bitten again!"

"Don't worry," her mother soothed. "Remember, this is my room, and neither your father nor I have a single bite on us."

Sighing, Kativa made herself lie back. Her mom left the room, and in only a few minutes Kativa fell soundly asleep.

But her dreams were terrible. She kept imagining the whole house as a giant web in which she was stuck, helplessly waiting to be eaten. And from somewhere, hiding from sight within the sticky, web-covered walls, there was the scrambling sound of something huge and hungry coming after her. Something on long pointed legs, with fangs like poison darts . . .

When she opened her eyes, after sleeping for almost three hours, Natasha was standing by her bedside.

"Hi, Tiva!" she sang out. "Now that you're awake, would you like to play?"

Kativa stretched and shook her head. "Natasha, I don't think I feel like playing right now," she said.

Natasha sighed. "You *never* have any time to play," she said in a pouty voice.

"Sorry," Kativa said, carefully checking her arms and legs. There were no new bites. "I've just got my mind on other things right now," she added.

Natasha brightened. "Mom says you talked to a crazy man at the college," she said.

Kativa smiled and sat up in bed. "Yes, I guess you could say that," she agreed. "He told us this weird story about how if you get bitten four times by this one spider you could turn into a spider yourself. Sounds nuts, doesn't it?"

But Natasha did not laugh. Instead, her face filled with concern. "Would you be scared if that was happening to you?" Natasha asked.

Kativa hadn't expected her sister to take her comments seriously. "That's *not* happening to me, Natasha," she

16

explained. Kativa tried to chuckle, just to show how ridiculous the idea was, but somehow she couldn't work up a laugh. She looked between the blinds, out the window. The sun was going down, and the sight made her feel even colder inside.

"Maybe that college man meant that it's kind of like a werewolf," Natasha pressed on, her eyes wide. "Except with *spiders* instead of wolves!"

Kativa finally found her voice. "Natasha, maybe we should stop talking about spiders, okay?"

Natasha looked at her sheepishly. "Sorry, Tiva," she said with a little shrug. Then she raced off. "Oh, by the way," she shouted back over her shoulder, "Mom wants you to come down for dinner if you feel up to it."

But Kativa wasn't hungry. All she could do was lie there, imagining that wherever she went in the house, spiders skulked behind potted plants and nestled in the valances on the tops of the curtains, ready to pounce on her.

....

That night her parents fixed up a cot for her in their own bedroom. They even plugged in her seashell night-light.

Her dad waved bravely at her just before rolling over to sleep. "Nothing will dare get you tonight," he promised. "Not with your father on duty!"

"Good night, dear," her mom said. "Just try to get some sleep, and I'm sure you'll feel much better in the morning."

Kativa sighed and rested her head on the pillow, but she was unable to sleep. She wished she hadn't taken such a long nap. She lay there, her eyes wide open in the darkness.

After a while she heard her parents lapse into even breathing, followed by light snoring. Kativa finally closed her eyes.

She was roused from sleep sometime later. A spider—*the* spider—was biting her, this time on the neck! Paralyzed with fear, Kativa forced her eyes open.

All she could see was Natasha's face looming before her. But something was terribly wrong. Fine black hair covered the little girl's features, and her eyes looked like furry black saucers. "It takes about a month, Tiva. Then you'll be like me," Natasha whispered, her voice like the high, screechy sound of violins being tuned. "Then we'll have *plenty* of time to play. Just think, we'll be two spiders, crawling through the house together after it gets dark!"

Kativa could not bring herself to make a sound. Nor could she move. Eight legs, all long and hairy, gripped her in a strong embrace. She could only watch as the changed face of her sister moved forward again to pierce her throat with its strawlike fangs.

Bloodmobile

Vince ran over the mossy forest floor, turning around to avoid a mammoth boulder. His timing was perfect: The Frisbee floated right into his waiting hands. "Can you *believe* we actually talked Mom and Dad into going camping in this beautiful place?" he yelled. He straightened his arm and hurled the yellow disc back in the direction from which it had come.

Vince's twin brother, Joe, made a mighty leap and snagged the Frisbee just before it would have sailed into their tent. "Yeah. We're lucky there's two of us," he said with a wink. "It makes it easier to wear them down." He tossed the Frisbee back to Vince, who turned and caught the plastic disc.

Vince held on to the Frisbee, looking at the trees towering overhead with a dreamy expression. "Just think of all the stuff we can do while we're here!" he said happily. "As soon as Mom and Dad get back from the camp store, we're going hiking, right? And in the morning we could go fishing or mountain biking. Then there's that campfire program tomorrow night . . ."

Joe rolled his eyes. "All right, man," he said with a grin. "It *is* pretty cool to be camping, but would you mind shutting up for a minute and just throwing the Frisbee back?"

Vince shot his twin a mock hurt expression. "Okay, but if you're going to be a jerk, you're gonna have to run for it!" he warned. He wound up and flung the Frisbee clear over to the next campsite. Joe snickered and shook his head, then turned to fetch the Frisbee. His eyes were scanning the thick underbrush for it when he came to a clearing and noticed an old, rusty camper parked under a gnarled oak tree. He examined the vehicle for a second before grabbing the Frisbee he'd spotted by the back tire. Then he sprinted back over to Vince, who was still standing by the huge boulder.

"Sorry about that throw," Vince said sheepishly.

"Never mind about that," Joe answered. He jerked a thumb over his shoulder. "Did you notice the beat-up motor home under that tree? I don't remember seeing it there yesterday."

Vince looked over. "They must've pulled in last night after we were already asleep," he suggested. "Why?"

"No reason," Joe said, trying to twirl the Frisbee on one finger. "It's just that it kind of smells funny over there, that's all."

"It smells 'funny'?" Vince exclaimed. "Like *what*?"

Joe only shrugged, and both boys stared silently over at the campsite. Just then their parents pulled up the dusty road in the family station wagon. Vince could practically taste the marshmallows, chocolate bars, and graham crackers hidden in the shopping bags in the backseat. The boys rushed over to help with the supplies.

"Well," their mom said, "who would like to do some hiking?"

"Me!" both boys responded at once.

············

The walk through the wilderness had not been disappointing. The boys had seen huge fir trees, giant oaks, a porcupine crossing a fallen tree, and, perhaps best of all, a raccoon that stopped and stared at the foursome before shimmying to the top of a tall pine tree. When the family got back to the campground, it was almost sunset. As they walked past the neighboring campsite, the twins glanced over at the old motor home, but nothing had changed.

"I wonder where they've been all day," Joe whispered to his brother.

Vince shook his head. "Maybe they're night people," he replied.

As their parents set up the camp stove and started dinner, Vince and Joe crept next door to have a closer look. They walked all around the vehicle, hoping that the curtains would be parted somewhere so they could peek inside, but every window was sealed up tight with thick black curtains. The boys walked off into the nearby forest.

"I see what you mean about the smell," Vince whispered with a little look of disgust. "It smells like something's *rotting*. And did you notice? There are no rearview mirrors on that camper—not on the side, not even in the cab!"

Joe narrowed his eyes, looking back at the silent camper. "What kind of people don't have any mirrors on their car and sleep all day?" he wondered aloud.

Vince smiled mischievously. "Maybe our neighbors are vampires," he suggested in a spooky voice.

Joe was still staring at the motor home. "Whatever they are," he said, "let's keep an eye on them."

· · · · · · · · · · ·

That night, the twins lay still in their tent until they could hear their parents snoring from the tent next door. Then they popped their heads up and took turns peeking out their tent's small screened window.

After a little while they heard a long, creaking noise. Both of them crowded to see out the window.

The side door of the motor home opened, and two figures stepped out into the moonlight: a man and a woman. Their thin bodies moved in slow motion, and their skin reflected a deathly white glow against their black garments.

"Maybe they *are* vampires," Vince whispered, no longer feeling like it was a big joke. "How could we find out?"

"I know," Joe said. He began pawing through his backpack, which sat in the corner of the tent. After a few seconds he came out with a pocket mirror.

They held the mirror up to the window and took turns adjusting it so they could see outside. When they looked directly through the window, they could see the weird, bony couple standing motionless under the moon. But when they looked in the mirror, all they could see was some black clothing, which appeared to float in the air. *The people who had come out of the camper cast no reflection.*

Panic-stricken, Vince looked at his twin. *"Now* what do we do?" he whispered.

"I have no idea," Joe answered. "But we'd better not let them out of our sight! We'll tell Mom and Dad in the morning."

But when they turned back to the window, their neighbors were nowhere to be seen.

....

The twins spent a nearly sleepless night, watching the mobile home through their tiny tent window. At any moment they expected the front of their tent to be slashed open by sharp claws, followed by two pale forms flying in through the new opening. But all they did see was the lonely forest, with the needles of the pine trees shimmering ever so softly in the white moonlight.

The boys were starting to nod off when they heard a familiar creak, followed by the sound of a door shutting. They both came to attention and stared out the window, but they were too late. Their neighbors were already inside.

....

"Get up, sleepyheads!" their father said, sticking his face into their tent. "It's almost eight o'clock! You're missing a beautiful morning!"

The boys groaned and rolled over in their sleeping bags. "I don't think I've ever been so tired," Vince said after their dad left.

Joe flopped onto his belly and propped his head up with one hand. "We've got to do something. What if they travel around, feeding on campers . . ."

"I wonder if they've gotten anyone in *this* campground yet," Vince said, sitting up at the thought. "If they have, then they might have created new vampires. We won't stand a chance if there are more than two."

Joe frowned, looking out their window at the solitary motor home. "I kind of doubt they've bitten anyone yet," he said. "Did you notice how thin they were?"

"They just got here, so they probably haven't started yet," Vince agreed. "So what do we do?"

"We need to get into their motor home to gather evidence to show Mom and Dad," Joe said firmly. "And we need to do it sometime today, while the sun is still up."

Vince nodded nervously. At the thought of their frightening mission, neither of the boys felt sleepy any longer. They wriggled out of their bags and got dressed.

· · · · · · · · · · ·

"What should we do today, you two?" their mother asked over a breakfast of scrambled eggs and bacon. "Want to go fishing? Or how about another hike?"

"I was thinking a picnic would be fun!" their dad suggested.

The twins looked at one another and swallowed. The same thoughts rushed through both of their heads. They knew they couldn't exactly tell their mom and dad they needed a little time to slip away and take care of a couple of vampires. Mom and Dad would never believe their story, anyway. And they realized their parents would get suspicious if they seemed disinterested in their plans—especially after all the begging that had led up to this trip.

"I'm up for anything!" Vince said with false cheer.

"Me, too!" Joe said. "Anything!"

The family finally decided to explore a nearby trail on their mountain bikes. They planned to make a day of it and packed picnic lunches. The twins exchanged helpless expressions at this turn of events, but neither of them could think of a way out.

So off they went, all four of them, riding through shady mountain meadows and past tranquil, tree-fringed streams. They found a path that traversed the very ridge of the mountains, and at lunchtime they stopped at a spot where they could see for miles on either side. The forest seemed to spread out away from them in a rolling green carpet of trees. It was the kind of adventure that the twins had been dreaming of for years.

Not that either one was able to enjoy himself. The mental image of that rusty motor home was never too far from their thoughts.

As the afternoon wore on, both boys began stealing nervous glances at the sky. The sun always went down early in the mountains, and they knew time was rapidly running out. Soon the vampires would be stalking for prey.

At last their parents aimed the bikes back toward the campground. Most of the early part of the day they had traveled slightly uphill—now they raced back down. The twins, anxious to return, took the lead and set roller-coaster speeds. Their mother shouted at them a number of times to slow down.

Finally they reached the campsite. The sun still hung in the sky, but it was already touching the tops of the pines. "Let's tell them we want to take a nap!" Vince whispered, just before their parents pulled up. "Maybe that'll give us a chance to sneak away!"

"We're worn out. How about a little nap before dinner?" Joe asked their mom and dad as they parked their bikes.

Their father laughed. "I'm not surprised you need to rest after the speed you were going!" he said. "I think a nap would be good for all of us."

"And that way we'll be well-rested for the campfire program tonight," their mother added.

The twins sighed in relief as everybody settled into their tents. They waited a few minutes, then moving as slowly and quietly as they could, they crept back out of their tent.

"The sun's almost down," Vince whispered. "We don't have much time."

They headed directly to the motor home, walking carefully so that the sound of crunching pine needles wouldn't give them away. Their hearts pounded as they stood before the side door of the camper. They both could imagine the pale-skinned couple standing right behind that door waiting to attack . . .

"Let's get this over with!" Vince whispered.

Joe nodded and grasped the door handle. Unlocked, it turned in his hand, and the door began to creak as it opened. The twins winced at the shrill noise, then both stepped bravely into the gloom.

"I can't see a thing!" Joe complained in a low voice.

Vince looked about, but his eyes weren't adjusting to the darkness. He tried a light switch by the door, but nothing happened. "The electricity must be disconnected," he whispered. "Let's open the drapes."

They proceeded to opposite windows, feeling their way blindly through the room. Joe bumped something flat and hard in the center of the room. He reached out and felt a long wooden box. *It has to be a coffin*, he thought in terror. *An occupied coffin!* He quickly moved away to where he thought the windows would be. Both boys reached the curtains at the same time, and tried to tug them open, but they wouldn't budge. The fabric had been nailed into place.

Suddenly there was a stirring noise from the center of the dark vehicle.

"Hurry!" Vince yelled, no longer bothering to speak quietly. "Force the drapes open!"

The boys pulled frantically on the curtains, but they still wouldn't move.

The stirring grew louder. A thin squeaking announced the opening of a lid.

The twins frantically pulled at the drapery with all their weight. All at once there was a ripping sound, as first Vince's and then Joe's curtain came tearing off the wall. The boys stared at the center of the room, where two red-eyed creatures were rising from a pair of black coffins. But something was different about them tonight. They were plump, not thin—and blood was smeared on each of their faces like fresh strawberry jam.

The creatures flew from their caskets like jack-in-the-boxes, one reaching for Vince and the other for Joe. But just before the vampires could touch them, the light shifted and the last dying rays of afternoon sunlight streamed through the window and fell upon them. Instantly, there was a sickening, burning smell in the motor home, and the creatures' red eyes rolled back into their heads. Horrid shrieks tore from their fanged mouths as their pale skin blackened and fell off in smoking scraps. In another instant their bones collapsed and turned into seething ashes on the floor.

Shuddering in fear and revulsion, the twins bolted out the door and into the forest. Darkness had shrouded the campsite.

Suddenly a hand fell on each of their shoulders. Both twins screamed and backed away, but it was only their father. Their mom stood next to him, her hands on her hips.

"You two have some explaining to do!" their dad said angrily.

Their mom stepped closer. "What were you doing in that motor home?" she snapped. "And what's that burning smell?"

"We'll tell you everything," Joe cried, "but first let's get back to camp and pack up before it's too late!"

Their parents looked at him as if he'd gone crazy.

"What are you talking about?" their mom added. The boys blurted out the whole story, emphasizing the part about the blood smeared over the vampires' faces.

"Now the important thing is for us to get out of here!" Vince said.

"Yeah!" Joe added. "Because those . . . things were full of blood before the sunlight killed them. They might have turned someone else around here into a vampire!"

Their father rubbed his chin thoughtfully. "I don't know how much of this I believe," he finally said, "but I do agree with one thing. I think we should go home before spending one more night here."

Behind him, their mom nodded her agreement.

The family struck the tents and packed things up as quickly as they could, since it was almost completely dark. By the time the twins were sitting in the backseat of the station wagon and their parents had taken their places in the front, a full moon had risen over the pines along the ridge, shining cold white light on the trail the family had ridden earlier that day on their mountain bikes. For the first time in nearly 24 hours Vince was beginning to feel normal again. He leaned forward and said to his parents, "Thanks for believing us, guys."

"Yeah," said Joe, slapping a hand on his father's shoulder. "No one else would have believed . . ." Smiling, he glanced at his dad in the rearview mirror and felt the blood rush out of his legs.

His father cast no reflection.

Joe leaned forward and grabbed the mirror, angling it in his mother's direction. She, too, was absent in the oblong mirror.

Bone Girl

here are they? Robin wondered, tightly holding onto the straps of her school backpack. She studied the street ahead as she walked, trying to pick out their hiding place. *Behind that car in the next driveway? Under the low hedge bordering the yard across the street?*

She only had to take a few more steps before she found out. Suddenly, a boy's voice rang out from behind the fence she was passing. "Hey, Bone Girl!" the kid yelled. "Why don't you get some flesh to cover those bones of yours?" The outburst was followed by a short chorus of giggles, then the sound of feet racing away from the fence and cutting across the yard to the next street.

Robin sighed and shook her head, never once slowing her steady stride. Who had it been this time? Brian Clark? Rosie Redland? It could have been any of them. Every day, either on the way to school or on the way home, it was the same thing. A certain group of kids would sneak up and try to scare her or tease her about the bones. Robin would have done anything to stop them, but she knew that once you had a nickname like "Bone Girl," it was pretty hard to shake.

After another few houses, she made a sharp turn and marched past the neglected roses and up the brick walkway of her home. She fished a key out of her jumper pocket and let herself into the "Bone House." At least that's what those kids called it.

There was good reason, too. Robin's living room was full of animals, birds, and people—just their bones, that is. Each skeleton hung from a special support. The smaller skeletons—those of squirrels, cats, and foxes—rose from tiny poles mounted on platforms. The larger ones, such as the gorilla and the human, hung from strings dangling from customized hangers, making them look like huge white marionettes. Higher, lined up along the ceiling as if trying to reach some ghoulish nest, the bones of birds in flight hung suspended from thin, strong wire.

Occasionally Robin would spot a town kid standing across the street, trying to catch a glimpse into the Bone House. She could never understand why anyone would care, but she couldn't understand her father's fascination for studying skeletons, either. "Don't look at them like that!" he always said when he caught her sneering at one of his precious "specimens," as he liked to call them. "You have to respect them!"

Remembering his words, Robin made a sound like escaping steam. *Sure,* she thought. *Like you can really respect a roomful of dead things.* Ignoring the cold stares the creatures cast at her from their eyeless sockets, she marched right past them and into the kitchen to prepare an afternoon snack.

In a few minutes she sat at the table, munching on a tuna sandwich. Not two feet from her chair stood the bones of a timber wolf, its sharp fangs glinting in the warm light slanting through the kitchen window. On a wall right over the table itself, in a decorative display case, lay coiled the fragile skeleton of an eight-foot rattlesnake. Robin dug hungrily into her sandwich, not giving the skeletons a second glance.

When she was through, she headed into the study. There she curled up on the couch located between the fearsome, towering skeletons of a pair of grizzly bears and did her homework.

At about six o'clock her dad came home. He wandered into the study, carrying a big box, and stared at Robin with a distracted expression. With his frizzy gray hair and thick glasses, he looked like the absentminded professor he was. Actually, Dr. Tim Meza was a scientist for the county museum.

"You won't believe what I picked up today!" he said, nodding toward the box in his arms. With infinite care he set it on the carpet, then slowly split the box's seal with a pocketknife. The box was filled with styrofoam packing material. Ever so gently, he reached in and withdrew the mounted skeleton of a bobcat, setting it down on the floor at their feet.

"Real cool, Dad," Robin said, boredom in her voice.

Her father didn't seem to notice her disinterest. Instead, he spent the next 15 minutes lecturing her on the bobcat's marvelous skeleton, pointing out how perfectly it was adapted for hunting with its large jaws, wide hindquarters, and thick leg bones. All the while Robin just nodded tiredly. She had heard it all before.

"Dad?" she said when he had finally finished. "I need some fatherly advice."

He blinked, and looked at her curiously. "Advice?"

"Yes," she said. "There's a group of kids at school who are teasing me. They call me Bone Girl, and—"

"Oh, they're probably just scared of my collection," her dad scoffed. "People are always scared of what they don't understand."

"Well, what do you suggest I do about it?" Robin wanted to know.

Her father shrugged. "*Educate* your friends about skeletons. After they learn a few things, they won't be scared any longer . . ." His voice trailed off and he tenderly picked up the bobcat, looking about the study for a good place to put it.

Robin brightened. "That just might work!" she said, turning it over in her mind. "Maybe I can bring some of the kids by the house. Once they see the skeletons up close, maybe they won't be so scared of them!"

Her father's attention was suddenly riveted on Robin. "Here?" he asked, stunned. "You want to bring a group of children through this house to gawk at my collection?"

"Well, you said . . ." Robin spluttered.

"I was thinking you could give your friends a little lecture at school or something!" he said sharply. "But bringing a crowd here would turn this house into a circus sideshow! That would most certainly *not* be treating the skeletons with respect. Don't forget what I've always told you, Robin: Skeletons must be treated with respect!"

With that, Dr. Meza marched into the front room, holding his new bobcat skeleton as gently as one might carry a carton of eggs.

....

The next day Robin sat in her history class staring blankly at the blackboard. The teacher was reviewing the reign of Alexander the Great, but Robin hadn't heard a word he said. She was too busy pondering her problem: how to get certain people to know her as Robin, instead of Bone Girl. She thought of her father's advice and tried to imagine herself marching to the front of the class to give a nice lecture about skeletons to everyone. *Yeah, right, Dad,* she thought, shaking her head.

Suddenly Robin was aware that Rosie Redland, who sat at the next desk, was watching her. Rosie was one of the leaders of the group that tormented her. Others were also looking in her direction, but when Robin turned to catch their gaze, they glanced away, snickering. She guessed what was going on. After all, she'd seen those knowing expressions often enough. Someone in the group had played a joke on her, and the others were waiting for her to discover it. They seemed to be staring down at the notebook under her fingers, so Robin figured out that something had been placed inside it. It wouldn't be the first time they had slipped a cruel note into her notebook.

At the front of the classroom, the teacher droned on about Alexander's wonderful empire while no one listened. Instead, most of the class was watching Robin, and Robin was trying to decide what to do. The smartest thing would probably be to check her notebook later so she wouldn't be giving any of them the satisfaction of seeing her reaction. She glanced at the closed cover. *What had they put in there, anyway?*

She held off as long as she could, but the suspense was too much. She quickly opened the notebook to find a crude cartoon drawing of a skeleton. It was holding a little bag marked "Candy." There was writing at the top of the page as well. "Hey, Bone Girl," it said. "We can guess what you're going to be for Halloween!"

A whisper of amusement went through the room. Robin knew if she looked now, the others in the group would be nudging each other and grinning. But for once, she didn't care, and she almost couldn't keep from grinning herself. The picture had given her the perfect idea.

She looked up at the calendar on the wall and began to count down down how many days were left until Halloween.

· · · · · · · · · · ·

"I'm going to be gone for three days next week," Robin's father told her that night. The pair were sitting in the living room, lightly dusting the skeletons with soft rags. It was a weekly ritual. "I've got a museum convention."

Usually such an announcement would have upset Robin. She hated it when her dad went away to his little bone

36

conventions, leaving her alone for days at a time. Her father was kind of a forgetful man, and she sometimes worried that he'd get so wrapped up studying his skeletons that he'd forget all about her and never come home at all. Tonight, however, none of that bothered Robin. In fact, as far as she was concerned, her dad's timing couldn't have been better.

"Which days will you be gone?" Robin asked casually. She had been dusting the huge, grinning crocodile skull on the floor, and her hand paused now as she waited for his answer.

Her father frowned. "I . . . don't remember," he said. He groped for a paper in his shirt pocket and pushed his glasses down on his nose so he could read through his bifocals. "Looks like the twenty-ninth, thirtieth, and thirty-first. I'll be back the morning of the first."

"Great!" Robin blurted out. Then, noticing her father's surprised expression, she added, "I mean, I'll miss you. What will you be studying this time?"

He thought for a second. "Oh, it's a seminar on the various foods that strengthen bones!" he beamed. And he proceeded to give her a little lesson on the subject right on the spot. His hands smoothed down his wild hair as he spoke. Robin listened halfheartedly for a few minutes until she had finished dusting the croc skeleton, then she excused herself to do her homework.

But when she got upstairs to her room, she didn't open her schoolbooks at all. Instead, she turned on her computer and opened up a graphics program. She typed away for nearly an hour, experimenting with different typestyles and inserting illustrations. Finally she was done. Robin took the first copy off the printer and studied it.

**TRICK OR TREAT PARTY AT THE BONE HOUSE!
COME TO ROBIN MEZA'S PLACE ON
HALLOWEEN NIGHT AT 6:00
FOR A PARTY YOU'LL NEVER FORGET
. . . IF YOU DARE!**

Robin smiled at the finished product. Yes, this would do. After this challenge, there wouldn't be a single kid in the group who would dare *not* to come. She got out a box of envelopes and began addressing them.

....

Robin had a feeling her father was right about people being scared of what they don't understand, so her number-one goal was to show them the skeletons close up. She didn't plan on giving any of her father's usual talks on how skeletons are the infrastructure of the body itself, or about what a marvel it is how one part of the body so perfectly supports another part. Kids would not be interested in learning stuff like that, especially on Halloween. All she wanted to do was give them a little scare, then show them how harmless her father's collection was. She hoped that then they'd stop calling her Bone Girl.

Finally Halloween night arrived and Robin was ready. She took a last look around the house to make sure everything was in place, then she checked her watch. It was almost six o'clock! Excited—and a little nervous—Robin ran to the front door where she watched for her guests out of the peephole.

Soon she saw a cluster of classmates wandering up the walk. Robin smiled. All eight of the kids she'd invited had come! She watched as they looked this way and that, noticing the fake webs and giant rubber spiders she had put in the rose bushes. Then they walked up to the front porch and stopped dead.

Robin smiled. Although she couldn't quite see what was going on because of the angle of the little peephole in the door, she knew they had come upon her first big surprise. There, crouched in the shadows by the doorbell, she had carefully set up the towering gorilla skeleton. Cradled in its long finger bones was a carved jack-o'-lantern, a candle flickering inside. Carrying the gorilla out had been a real chore, and she still remembered the way its huge jaw had come loose and flapped up and down as she moved it. She had imagined it was a live animal trying to snap at her.

Robin watched as the kids finally turned to knock on the door, and she eagerly opened it. Rosie Redland was the first one inside. "Great pumpkin holder," she said, nodding at the gorilla on the porch.

"Thanks," Robin said. It was the first compliment Rosie had ever paid her. Robin smiled and faced the other guests. "Come on in, everyone," she said. "And I'll show you around the Bone House!"

Robin shut the door behind them, taking in the kids' surprised expressions as they looked about. She had hoped they would react like this. She'd entirely draped the walls of the front room with torn trash bags, stapled end-to-end and hanging from the wooden beams of the ceiling. The effect created a dark, mysterious space, with only chairs and a card table in sight.

Robin moved to one wall. The kids followed her, wide-eyed, wondering what she had planned. She grabbed hold of a section of the overhead trash bags. "First, these are some of the family pets!" she announced. And with a sharp tug, she wrenched several of the bags loose. They fell like a theater curtain, revealing a few feet of the wall and floor beyond.

The others stared.

Before them stood some of the smaller skeletons, such as the squirrels and the cats. Around each of their necks Robin had attached a collar and leash, and there were some old dog bowls on the floor. The stark white bones caught the light and glimmered. The little scene looked like a kennel of ghost animals.

"Whoa!" Brian Clark exclaimed. "I've always wondered—are . . . are these things *real* skeletons, Robin?"

"Of course!" she said. "My dad is Dr. Meza. He's an expert on skeletons at the museum, so he always keeps a bunch of them at home to study."

The others nodded uncertainly, and Robin led them further into the room. "Enough of the animals for now. How would you like to meet a human skeleton?" She watched as the kids' eyes grew wider. Before they could answer, she ripped away another section of the trash bags to unveil the adult male skeleton. She had placed a top hat from her father's closet on its head and draped a cape about its shoulder bones. The group was speechless. But Robin wasn't about to stop there. "You've always called me Bone Girl just because we have all these skeletons in our house. Now you can see what a real 'bone person' looks like!" she said teasingly.

"The skeleton is a symbol of death," Rosie finally said. "Doesn't it kind of give you the creeps, living in a house with so many of them?"

"Naw," Robin answered truthfully. "They do look a little weird at first, but they can't hurt you. Look, I'll prove it. Come and shake its hand—unless you're afraid!"

Rosie paused for a second, then bravely reached out and grasped the skeleton's fingers. Quickly, she drew her hand away and wrinkled her nose. Then a grin filled her face. "Weird. It feels like cold wood!"

"Oh, let me try next," Monica Atwood begged.

"Then me," added Brian Clark.

"Wow!" Monica said a second later. "Bones really *do* feel like cold wood!"

Robin stood back, enjoying her moment of victory. The kids were actually standing in line for a chance to shake the skeleton's hand! A second later, however, the smile faded from her face. When she glanced up at the human skull, she thought she noticed some strange shadows flicker in the deep hollows of its eye sockets. But that was ridiculous, she decided. The illusion must have been created by the shadows of her party guests.

In a few minutes Robin led the kids to the chairs and told them to sit. "I thought we could play a party game," she said. "Who wants to go first?"

A boy named Alex raised his hand. Robin noticed that he had been the last one to touch the skeleton, and she figured he now wanted the others to think he wasn't scared. "Okay, Alex," Robin said. "Take this." She pressed a length of small bones, all joined by a thin wire, into Alex's palm. A gummy wad of something clung to the bone at one end.

"Wha-what's this?" he asked, horrified.

"It's just a *tail*," Robin said casually, "with some gum on it to make it stick." She walked off and yanked back all of the trash bags at the end of the room. Against the far wall was the skeleton of the timber wolf, its sharp teeth menacing. It was missing its tail. "Here. Put this over your eyes," Robin said, tossing a bandanna to Alex. "It's time to play Stick the Tail on the Timber Wolf!"

Alex obediently blindfolded himself, and the others spun him around. He tottered hesitantly across the room, holding out the tailbone with shaking fingers. He grew especially nervous when he drew close to the standing bones of the wolf, and he attached the tail to the first thing he felt. When he removed the bandanna, he saw the tail dangling from the wolf's jaw. The others chuckled weakly.

"That wasn't too good, Alex," Robin scolded. "Well? Who's next?"

For the next half hour or so, the kids took turns being blindfolded and groping around the room with the tailbone. The group was quiet at first, but by the end everyone was hooting and laughing.

"Good tries, everyone!" Robin said. "Now, anybody for some . . . refreshments?" And with that, she reached up and tore away all of the remaining trash bags.

Beyond were the rest of her father's specimens, posed in ways that he never would have imagined in his worst nightmares. The huge yellowish bones of a grizzly bear held out a punch bowl filled with fruit juice and ice. At its feet, the thin bones of the rattlesnake curled about a tower of paper cups. The fox skeleton and the bobcat balanced platters of candy in their jaws, and next to them loomed the other grizzly bear, holding a tin of cookies in one fleshless paw and a stack of paper plates in the other.

Even Robin had to admit to herself that the scene she had created was unbelievably weird. But by now her party guests were growing used to the sights in the Bone House. Most of them just chuckled appreciatively and went forward to sample the treats.

"Do you have any napkins, Robin?" Alex asked.

She smiled. "Sure," she said. "But you'll have to jump for them." She pointed up, where a line of skeleton birds hovered just overhead. Each one had a napkin in its beak. The kids laughed again, shaking their heads, and began bounding into the air for their napkins.

"You thought of everything," Alex said grinning.

Soon the food was gone and Robin's party guests had to leave. They were all kinder to Robin than they'd ever been before, and each one thanked her for an unforgettable Halloween party. At last the crowd headed out to the porch. Rosie was the last one out. "Hey, Robin," she said, patting her on the shoulder. "We always thought you were kind of weird, but you're all right, girl."

Robin shut the door, raising both fists into the air. "Yes!" she said. The night had gone *exactly* as she had planned! She peered out the peephole again so she could watch the group heading down the walk. They wouldn't be bothering her anymore. She had neatly solved her problem.

Robin watched until her new friends passed out of sight into the dark Halloween night. She sighed happily. Now it was time to clean up. Her dad might not think she'd been exactly "respectful" of his collection if he saw it the way it was now. Robin chuckled.

Turning from the door, Robin bent down to pick up a trash bag at her feet, but all at once she straightened up, alarmed. Her eyes blinked, over and over, as she stared out at the front room.

The trash sacks lay wadded on the floor, the table and chairs stood just as they had been, and the empty punch bowl and crumpled paper plates lay scattered on the table. But the special support stands were all empty! *There was not one skeleton anywhere in the room.*

"Hey," Robin said, frowning. "What's going on?"

Out of the corner of her eye she saw a pale blur of motion coming at her. She turned, but before she could focus on it the lights were snuffed out. A hollow, almost musical sound seemed to be surrounding her. *That sounds like wind chimes,* she thought in confusion. *Or bones, clinking together . . .*

Suddenly she felt things clutching at her—hard, clawlike things, plucking at the skin of her arms and her neck and her face.

The things felt very much like cold wood.

....

The next morning Dr. Meza let himself into his house.

"I'm home!" he shouted. There was no answer. *That's funny. Where is that daughter of mine?* he wondered.

He set down his suitcases and walked into the front room. Everything seemed okay—the room was clean and all the skeletons were in their places.

He rounded the corner. "Robin Muriel?" he yelled, using her full name. Dr. Meza stuck his head into the study. She wasn't there, either, but all his specimens were just where they should be.

In the hall, he stopped, surprised, combing his fingers through his gray hair.

A new skeleton stood before him. It was set up on a stand, right at the base of the stairs. The faintly pink bones appeared to be those of a human girl, but for the life of him, Dr. Meza could not remember when or where he got it.

Things from the Jungle

At last Benjamin was finished sweeping. He scooped up the plant clippings, spilled fertilizer and planting soil, and deposited them in a big trash bag. Now all he had left to do was empty the wastebaskets. He took a second to look nervously around the nursery—especially into the mysterious green shadows behind him—then allowed himself a little break, leaning on his broom. His eyes wandered over the plants filling the nursery, and finally settled on the big sign bolted to the beam overhead, lit up in neon so that people could see it at night through the store's front window.

THINGS FROM THE JUNGLE, the sign read, a pale green glow reflecting off the glass.

The name had been his mother's idea. Everything had been her idea. "Just think, Benjamin," she'd said only two years ago, "a nursery, stocked with exotic plants shipped directly from Africa! This town is *filled* with wealthy people who'll pay top dollar for something really unusual to put in their yards." And she had been right, of course. Even though there were just the two of them to run it, THINGS FROM THE JUNGLE had been successful since the day it opened.

Benjamin sighed, then looked behind him again into the huge warehouse where the plants were stored and cared for. It looked like a jungle, all right, with colorful flowers everywhere, vines looping from fluffy bushes, and banana trees rising over it all. When his mom looked back there, all she saw was money. But when Benjamin looked back at the vast leafy space—especially now, at night, when the thick plants seemed to go on forever—he always had the same strange thought: *Something is watching me.*

Benjamin had that feeling now. He found himself staring into the green shadows, half expecting a pair of predatory eyes to glint back at him. He shook his head and put the broom and dustpan back into the closet. *Grow up*, he chided himself. *There's nothing back there.* But, as usual, trying to be logical did no good at all, and he quickly finished emptying the wastebaskets and headed out the front door.

Relieved to be finished, Benjamin took a deep breath of the crisp air outside the warehouse. Then he took the trash sack to the open Dumpster out back. But as he hefted the bag over the lip of the Dumpster, he saw a strange shadow out of the corner of his eye. A man was standing motionless just to the side of the Dumpster.

"Chester!" Benjamin yelled when he saw who it was. "You almost scared me to death!"

Chester shrugged, toyed with a strand of his long white hair, then slowly walked away down the alley. As he watched the old man, Benjamin supposed every neighborhood had a homeless guy like Chester—he just wished that this one didn't have to spend so much time hanging around the nursery.

Benjamin closed the Dumpster's lid and walked the 50 feet between the family business and the family home: a small, single-level house he and his mom had lived in ever since she opened THINGS FROM THE JUNGLE.

Inside was evidence of his mother's green thumb. Every surface, from the television to the refrigerator, was covered with the potted plants she had personally grown from clippings in the nursery. The little plants, miniature versions of the huge untamed ones in the warehouse, made Benjamin's home look like a jungle, too.

"Everything all cleaned up out there, Ben?" his mother called out.

Benjamin came into the den to join her. She was sitting at their craft table, her fingers working to pack a little green vine into the soil of a ceramic pot.

"Yeah, Mom," he answered. "It's all ready for the morning."

His mother dribbled some water onto the newly potted plant from a watering can, then set it aside. Finally she pulled off a paper towel to wipe the planting soil from her fingers. "Well, I'm going to turn in," she said, nodding up at the wall clock. "There's a truck coming in early tomorrow and I have to open the warehouse for the drivers to unload the new plants."

After exchanging a good-night kiss, they both retired to their bedrooms.

But Benjamin had trouble falling asleep. He couldn't stop thinking of the big semi trucks that brought new exotic plants and trees to the nursery once a month. He knew these trucks loaded up from boats that came directly from Africa. But he'd always had a weird suspicion that the shipments sometimes contained a little more than the plants he and his mom had ordered.

After tossing and turning for about an hour, Benjamin lay on his side, staring off through his window at the nursery warehouse. Even from here it felt as if something inside were watching him from behind the dark windows.

Watching . . . and waiting.

• • • • • • • • • • •

When Benjamin got home from school the next afternoon, the entire nursery looked different. They had received an unusually large shipment, with so many plants arriving on the truck that even the huge warehouse couldn't hold them all. The overflow spilled out into the small showroom near the front door and even into his mom's tiny office at the side. Everywhere he looked was a mass of green: curling green ferns, low flats of twisting green grasses, and green trees hanging with strange fruits.

His mom's face peeked from between a pair of shaggy bushes. "Hi, Ben!" she said with an exhausted but happy smile. "Boy, have we been busy! With all these new plants, I've been hooking up extensions to the drip lines all day! And look at all the customers!"

Benjamin nodded. There was quite a crowd of people wandering through the place, admiring the new arrivals. Word always seemed to get out whenever THINGS FROM THE JUNGLE received a new shipment. "Give me a few minutes to put my school stuff away," he told her, "and I'll be right out to help you."

"Thanks, honey," she said, winking at him. "I knew I could count on you."

When Benjamin came back out, Mrs. Girrard was the first customer to catch his eye. "There you are, Ben!" the plump older woman said. "I've been waiting for you!" She lived only two blocks away and had been one of their regular customers from the very beginning. About twice a month she walked to the nursery, purchased a plant or two, then sent her husband to pick them up by car later. Mrs. G., as she liked to be called, waved her hand about the room. "I've never seen this place so full of greenery!" she exclaimed. "Would you be a dear and show me some of the new things?"

Benjamin smiled and directed Mrs. G. around, bending to check a price tag on a dwarf fruit tree or to explain how to care for a flowering vine. His mom had taught him quite a bit about plants and he could identify almost every shrub in the place. Finally Mrs. G. stopped him. "I love everything you've shown me!" she said. "But I can't buy them all. Let me have a few minutes alone to think about it, will you?"

Benjamin nodded, watching as she strolled off into the warehouse, a wistful smile on her face. Then he went off to help a new customer.

They finally closed at six o'clock. After the doors were shut and the Open sign was turned around, Benjamin's mom looked at him and raised her eyebrows. "I've got a good feeling about this," she said, turning with a dramatic flourish and pushing the button that opened the cash register drawer. She reached in and took a minute to count the cash inside. Then she looked up. "We just had a record day, Ben!" she beamed. She took the money and slipped it into a folder, then reached over to affectionately tousle Benjamin's hair. "Thanks for all your help," she grinned. "Tell you what—what if you do a real quick cleanup tonight while I deposit this money at the bank? Then I'll pick up a pizza on my way home. I think we deserve it!"

While his mother was gone, Benjamin became lost in his work. As he swept up the fallen leaves, his mind mulled over the day's activities and his stomach rumbled with the thought of a pizza dinner. But somewhere near the very rear of the warehouse, where the plants were so thick you couldn't see one sign of civilization, he stopped cold.

High in the trees overhead he heard a distinct rustling noise. It sounded as if some large animal was suddenly moving from branch to branch. Benjamin stared up in wonder, expecting to see . . . what? Nothing except the usual canopy of jungle trees greeted his eyes.

The noise stopped, just as suddenly as it had begun.

Benjamin looked around the huge, plant-filled space. He was certain he was not alone. But no matter how long he paused, his heart booming in his chest, the noise did not repeat itself. The only things he could hear were the crickets sawing away in the darkness outside and the occasional light *whooshing* sounds of the timed drip lines going off at various parts of the warehouse to water the plants.

Finally Benjamin gathered his courage and finished his sweeping. Then, with shaking hands, he turned off the warehouse lights, locked up, and walked home.

....

In the middle of their pizza dinner, the phone rang. Benjamin watched his mom's smile melt from her face during the conversation. At the end of the conversation she dropped the slice of pizza she had been eating onto her plate. It was clear she had lost her appetite.

"That was the police," she said, shaking her head in shock. "Mrs. Girrard's husband said that she never made it home this evening. They wanted to see if we knew anything about her. I told them she had been at the store, but that I hadn't seen her since about four o'clock."

Benjamin set down his pizza. He looked out the window toward the nursery, recalling the last sight he'd had of Mrs. G., strolling deeper into the warehouse. He hesitated before he spoke. When he did, he was surprised at his own words. "I wonder if the thing in the warehouse got her . . . "

Benjamin's mother stared at him in surprise. "What are you talking about?" she asked.

Benjamin took a deep breath. "I mean, for the longest time I've had this feeling that something's been . . . *living* in there. I didn't want to say anything because I didn't think you'd believe me, but tonight I heard this noise, way up in the branches . . . "

His mom stared at him in horror. "I wonder if something could have hitched a ride from Africa," she mumbled. "Like an animal—or a snake?"

Benjamin shrugged, wide-eyed.

"Maybe something attacked Mrs. Girrard!" she gasped. "Right in our nursery!" She picked up the phone again and called the police.

....

Two police cars pulled up a short while later and parked in front of the warehouse, emergency lights flashing. The officers told Ben and his mom to stay in their house. They sat silently in the living room, watching the red lights reflecting off the leaves of the potted plants surrounding them. Benjamin kept waiting for the sounds of gunfire, or a lion's roar, or even a cop yelling out, "There it is!" to the others. But nothing like that happened.

Finally they saw a tall policeman with a mustache making his way up to their house.

They opened the door for him, and he nodded and handed Benjamin's mother his business card. "We appreciate your calling us, and you can do it again if you think of something," he said politely, studying both Benjamin's and his mother's faces with his gray eyes. "But we searched every square foot in that building, and we couldn't find signs that anything more dangerous than a couple of mosquitoes are living in there. We're sure there must be some other explanation for Mrs. Girrard's disappearance."

Mother and son watched the police units pull away from the parking lot and drive off. Dazed, they wandered into the dining room. Benjamin looked sheepishly at his mother, who toyed with the cop's business card.

"Must have been my imagination, huh, Mom?" he said.

"I hope so. But it's good to be sure," she said. She slipped the card under their telephone and snagged the white box on the table. With a deft motion of one hand, she flipped open its lid. "Anyone for cold pizza?" she asked with a smile.

....

The next day was Saturday, and THINGS FROM THE JUNGLE was having another record day. By noon Benjamin had given brief tours to a schoolteacher, a hotel operator, several tourists, two gardeners, and one memorable family with three misbehaving redheaded kids. They had to put the Closed sign up at one o'clock so Benjamin and his mother could take a few minutes out for lunch.

They sat in her office while both munched on leftover pizza. Ben's mom had wanted to take their break in the nursery so she could go over the sales receipts while they ate. Benjamin sighed and listened idly to the ticking noise from her calculator. *Thank goodness we're closed on Sundays,* he thought. *We're going to need a day to just sit and—*

Suddenly his thoughts were interrupted by a loud rustling noise swishing through the branches somewhere in the warehouse. It was just like the sound Benjamin had heard the previous night. Something huge seemed to be leaping from tree to tree. He stopped chewing. His mother stopped typing. Both stared at each other, speechless.

The noise stopped.

Mother and son walked carefully out of the office, looking about the nursery with bulging eyes. Everything seemed normal.

"Did you hear it?" Benjamin whispered.

"Yes," she said. Then, turning to face the warehouse, she called out, "Is there anyone in here?"

The only sound was the traffic rushing by outside.

....

That night a knock fell on the nursery's front door just after closing time. It was the same mustached policeman who had visited them the previous evening.

"I'm terribly sorry to be bothering you again," he said as they opened the door. "But we've had a report that some other people have disappeared."

"Other people? Disappeared?" Benjamin's mother asked, confused. "What does that have to do with us?"

"Well, I stopped by because I noticed that their vehicle appears to be parked in your parking lot." He pointed out the window at a dented minivan parked there. With all the traffic in and out of their little lot all day, neither of them had noticed it.

Benjamin's mom clapped her hand over her mouth in surprise. Benjamin just stared, a strange idea coming into focus in his mind. "What do they look like?" he asked quietly.

The officer took out a snapshot and held it up. Before them was a picture of a mother, father, and three redheaded children. His mom was starting to shake her head to indicate that she hadn't seen them, but Benjamin nodded. "Yes," he said quickly. "They were here. I showed them around, but they didn't buy anything. I . . . I thought they must have left."

A sharp look came into the policeman's gray eyes. "What time was this?"

Benjamin swallowed. "About eleven-thirty," he said. "Before lunch."

"Hmm. Mind if I look around the warehouse again?" the policeman asked.

"Please do!" his mother said.

Ben and his mother simply sat at the desk in the office, speechless. A mental film of the family replayed itself over and over again in Benjamin's head. A weird detail stuck in his mind. *Everyone in the family had worn bright yellow tennis shoes.* He went on to remember how all three redheaded kids kept taking off and running away from their exasperated parents. Had one of the little ones led the rest of them deeper into the warehouse? To that spot where the rustling noise kept coming from?

"I didn't see anything back there," the cop said, reappearing at the office door. "But those plants you have are so thick, it's kind of hard to tell." He looked toward the two and offered them a tight-lipped smile. "Look, it's possible their van wouldn't start after they came in here, and that they either walked or got a ride. I'll have to get back to you. You have my card—please call my number if they turn up." With that, he began walking toward the door.

Alarmed, Benjamin's mom stood up. "Is there anything else we can do?" she asked.

"Well, yes," the officer said, turning back toward them a final time. "Why don't you keep your nursery closed until we figure out exactly what's going on here?"

Benjamin's mother nodded grimly, and watched the tall policeman let himself out.

···········

That night Benjamin was restless again. For hours he simply lay on one side, staring out his window at the warehouse, different explanations flitting through his mind. At midnight Benjamin was still wide awake, and he noticed a long shadow moving in the alleyway at the side of the nursery.

He sat straight up in bed to see over the soft outlines of potted plants his mother had placed along his sill. Something was creeping toward the window near the warehouse door, approaching from the direction of the parking lot. In the midnight gloom Benjamin couldn't quite tell what it was, but whatever it was caused a chill to run through him.

He got out of bed and pressed his nose to the glass. A man was fiddling with the window. In another second he had taken the entire window off, and as he turned to lay it against the wall, a glint of moonlight stole through the clouds and lit up his face. Ben recognized the long white hair of Chester. Ben watched the old man climb through the window of the warehouse. *How long has Chester known how to get in that way?* Benjamin wondered. *Is he looking for a place to sleep—or does he have some other business in there?*

Benjamin quickly threw on some clothes. *Chester must be behind all the disappearances!* he thought excitedly. *But I'd better be sure before I drag the police out here again.*

Benjamin walked quietly through the dark house, took the key ring off the hook under the kitchen counter, then carefully slipped out into the moonlight.

Walking slowly, careful not to make a sound, Benjamin approached the warehouse window. At last he reached the sill Chester had climbed over to enter the warehouse. He hesitated, wondering if he dared go in that way. Chester could be right there, just waiting for him. Benjamin decided the door would be safer.

Ever so slowly Benjamin crept around to the front entrance and inserted the key in the keyhole. But when he turned the knob, it wouldn't give. Was someone holding the knob from the other side of the door? He tried again, and with a sigh of relief he realized that the key simply needed a little more pressure. In an instant the door swung open and he was inside the dark showroom.

Blinking, trying to adjust his eyes to the dimness, Benjamin could hardly see a thing through the thick masses of plants that absorbed any light coming through the windows. He had to get to the office and turn on the lights. Taking a deep breath, Benjamin walked toward the office, using his memory of how the building was laid out to find his way.

Plants seemed to reach out and touch him as he passed. At any second he expected a hand to grab at him out of the blackness. Finally he made it to the office. As he extended his hand toward the light switches, the familiar rustling noise swished through the warehouse—followed by a man's scream.

Benjamin jumped and his fingers flipped one switch. A single bank of lights flickered on, casting light on only one side of the warehouse.

The scream echoed out again, becoming muffled at the end.

Someone obviously needed help and needed it now. Forgetting about the rest of the lights, Benjamin entered the warehouse, squinting at the shadows. Something was moving wildly up ahead. Benjamin moved cautiously forward, looking up into the canopy of jungle trees. Then he saw something that made his heart stop.

A vine was pulling Chester up to the treetops.

Chester's feet and legs kicked and struggled in midair. The upper part of his body was entirely engulfed by the massive vine, which wrapped around his torso.

Benjamin, horrified, took a step back. Above him, hidden just under huge leaves, were other human shapes. They hung motionless in the clutching vines, just like plucked chickens. From the bottom of one particularly small bundle dangled a small pair of bright yellow tennis shoes.

Benjamin screamed. At the same time, the vines hauling up Chester paused, as if listening. A huge mass of vines, moving with incredible speed, suddenly dropped from the trees at the side of the warehouse. The action was accompanied by a loud rustling. They reached out and, with the precision of a giant's fist, smashed into the bank of lights Benjamin had turned on. The fluorescent tubes cracked like matchsticks, and the nursery went dark.

Benjamin looked around, gasping in shock. He could not see a thing. *Which way was it to the door?* He hesitated, turning this way and that, his sense of direction gone.

Above him the rustling sound grew louder still. Probing tendrils tickled his face. Suddenly a thicker vine moved up behind him and tried to loop itself around his throat. Tugging it away, Benjamin turned and plunged in the opposite direction.

Toppling over small trees, tripping over bushes, Benjamin ran through the pitch darkness. Vines crawled out after him the entire way, snatching at his legs, grabbing his arms, yanking his hair.

Finally the darkness parted, and he saw the moon, still riding high in the clouds, through the window. He had made it to the front of the building! Safety was only a few feet away. Still going full-speed, Benjamin yanked at the doorknob and tumbled down the front steps into the parking lot.

Panting and stunned, he lay there for a moment, thinking he had never seen anything as beautiful as the night sky overhead.

But the clatter of breaking glass filled the night around him. He stared in disbelief as three monstrous vines shot through the shattered window, coming after him. But only a few feet away, they abruptly stopped. Benjamin slowly realized that their roots anchored them from somewhere inside. Defeated, the pulsing stalks slithered, snakelike, back into the building.

Benjamin picked himself up and ran toward his house. It wasn't wild animals, and it wasn't other people, he thought, rehearsing what he would tell the cop on the phone. *Some weird kind of jungle plant was behind the disappearances!*

Benjamin let himself inside and hurried for the phone. He fished out the policeman's card and began dialing. But before he could reach the last number, something closed over one ankle.

As he kicked, trying to free himself, another tiny vine wrenched the phone receiver out of his hand. And another one grabbed his other arm. He looked around the room in amazement. The vines came from pots all around, the pots his mother had planted with clippings from the nursery. He turned to call for her, only to see that her bedroom door was open. Her body was covered with green vines, streaming from pots all around her bed. The body was not moving.

Benjamin's other leg was entrapped by the vines now, and a particularly big one was squeezing his chest. All of a sudden he could hardly move, but he found that he could scream.

And Benjamin kept screaming, right until the moment the vines wrapped themselves firmly over his mouth.

The Black Balloon

scar's parents started preparing for the party at about eleven in the morning.

First I saw them sweep the patio and clean off the outside chairs. Next his dad rigged up the piñata, hanging it from a hook in the porch ceiling. Then both his mom and dad started to twist streamers through the railings. They also stretched them in arcs from one end of the patio to the other.

They were really going all out for this birthday party, but I wondered why. Hadn't they ever stopped to consider what a little jerk their son was?

I sighed and went into my apartment for a soda. When I came out I sat down at the table on my own patio, and

63

looked around the complex. Most of the other patios had some signs of kids in the family: mountain bikes leaning against the walls, skateboards propped up by front doors. This complex was basically loaded with kids. And I knew for a fact that I was the only one of them *not* invited to Oscar's birthday party.

I grunted and took a sip of soda. What made the whole thing even worse was that both our apartments were on the ground floor, and mine was right across from Oscar's. That meant I could hear everything that would happen and I'd have a very clear view of the party. At first I planned to spend the day inside, but then I decided I would force myself to watch the entire event. If Oscar looked over and saw me sitting here with a bored expression on my face, maybe he'd realize that I wouldn't have wanted to come to his stupid party even if he *had* invited me.

After a few minutes his parents began setting up plastic chairs. Next they brought out card tables and decorated them with bright tablecloths. Finally his dad squirted lighter fluid over the coals in their portable barbecue and lit it so the coals would be ready by party time. Not once during all this preparation did I see Oscar himself. I supposed he was sitting in the house like a little king, waiting for his subjects to come and pay him respect.

I sipped my soda and waited.

A little before twelve-thirty the first guests arrived. I knew every one of them, either from school or here at the apartment complex. He'd invited both boys and girls. After a while I saw Tommy Robinson and Hank Melendez coming up the walk, both holding gifts. They were the buddies from my Little League team who had told me about Oscar's party to begin with. As they walked in his gate, they turned and waved at me. I tried to put a smile on my face as I waved back to them.

Finally the great boy himself came out of his house. I looked at Oscar's plump little face with a feeling of distaste. I had never liked him much. He was kind of a bully, the type of kid who picks on smaller kids and likes to boss people around. In fact, his meanness was the very reason we were enemies. Once I saw him kicking a neighbor's kitten, so I went and told the neighbor. Old Oscar got in a load of trouble over that, and he never forgave me. That was why he was over there having a party and I was over here, sitting alone on my porch.

I drained my soda can and crushed it, pretending it was Oscar's head.

The party went on predictably for a while. His dad put some burgers and hot dogs on the barbecue while the kids played some lame party games. They took a break to eat, then everyone lined up to whack at the piñata. When it was Oscar's turn I distinctly saw him peek under his blindfold before he swung the bat. Typical, I thought.

I was on my third soda before things started getting interesting.

That was when I saw the wizard walking down the central sidewalk of the complex. What he really was, of course, was an actor or an entertainer *dressed* like a wizard, but boy, did he have a great costume: a white beard that came down to the middle of his chest; long, flowing purple robes; and a peaked purple hat to match. And what an expression on his face! He looked as if he were ready to cast a spell on the first person who looked at him sideways.

As the wizard let himself in Oscar's gate, I was wishing for the first time that I *had* been invited to the party.

"Okay, everyone! The magician's here!" Oscar's mom announced. The kids finished scooping up the fallen piñata candy and sat on the chairs.

For a second the wizard just stared at them. Then he raised both hands in the air and clapped them twice. A spark and a great puff of smoke rose from between his fingers. When he spoke, his voice was deep and commanding. "I am Zatlin the Wizard. And"—the wizard stared at the faces in front of him before picking out Oscar—"you are Oscar, the birthday boy. Am I correct?"

Oscar rolled his eyes. "Good trick," he said sarcastically. "My parents must've shown you my picture, right?"

Zatlin frowned. "Do you doubt my magical powers?" he asked sternly.

Oscar snorted. "Anybody could wear a purple dress and set off some cheap fireworks," he said with a sneer. He looked around to see if any of his guests were laughing, but they were all ignoring him, eager to see what Zatlin would do next.

I wasn't laughing, either. I thought the magician was pretty impressive, and more than anything I was wishing he would turn Oscar into a frog or something.

The wizard continued to perform his tricks, and they were all good ones. He made doves appear from his fingertips, linked and unlinked rings, and made the birthday cake levitate in the air. After each trick, just like clockwork, Oscar made some rude comment.

For his last effect Zatlin made numerous helium balloons appear from under his cloak. I was completely amazed at that one. I couldn't figure out where he had been hiding them. But the trick got even more surprising after he handed a different colored balloon to each kid.

"Hey," Missy Johnson said. "How did you know green is my favorite color?"

Tommy Robinson smiled and held up his balloon. "Orange is mine! How did you *do* that, anyway?"

The wizard only smiled. The others all began to talk excitedly, everyone proclaiming that the magician had somehow managed to give them a balloon of their own favorite color. Finally he turned to Oscar, to whom he had given a bright red balloon. "Well?" Zatlin asked.

I saw Oscar's face kind of twist as he looked at his balloon. "Nope," he said. "You screwed up. My favorite color has always been blue."

At this the wizard turned away and began gathering up his doves and magic tricks. I could barely contain myself at that one. Oscar's bedroom was clearly visible from my place, and I knew he had red wallpaper and a red bedspread! Not only that, red-colored clothing was about the only thing he wore! He had lied, simply to make the magician look bad!

I watched as the wizard said his good-byes, and all the kids thanked him—except, of course, for Oscar, who was digging into his store of piñata candy. Then Zatlin let himself out the gate. But instead of leaving the way he had come in, he turned on his heel and came right across the courtyard toward my apartment.

I sat up in my chair, surprised to see that he seemed to be looking at me. The wizard strolled right up to my patio and stopped. He stared right into my eyes. I was a little shocked when I noticed that his beard and bushy white eyebrows were real.

"I liked your magic," I said awkwardly, trying to fill the silence. "And I know you were right about Oscar's balloon."

"Didn't you get invited?" Zatlin asked bluntly.

I could only shake my head. "Oscar and I aren't the best of friends," I mumbled.

The wizard's penetrating eyes seemed to consider me. All at once he reached into his cloak and brought out one more balloon. Its color was a shiny black. "I know this isn't your color, but I have a feeling it will liven up your afternoon," he said, carefully handing it to me. "Don't do anything you will regret," he added mysteriously. Then he turned with a swirl of his robe and strode up the sidewalk.

I simply sat there at first, shocked that he had approached me. Across the way, the birthday cake was being cut. No one at the party seemed to have noticed that I had been visited by the wizard.

I looked at the black balloon, wondering how in the world it was going to "liven up" my afternoon. I kind of wished he'd come up with a purple balloon. At least it would have been my favorite color.

Watching the kids eat their cake was pretty boring, so I amused myself making little squeaky noises by rubbing the top of the balloon.

Then I happened to look over at the party. Oscar was scratching at the top of his head, exactly where I'd been rubbing the balloon. I chuckled. What a weird coincidence.

I rubbed the balloon again. Oscar set down his fork on his cake plate and scratched at his head.

This was too strange. I stared at the balloon, trying to see if there was anything unusual about it, but all I could see was a normal, black rubber balloon tied with kite string.

Then I rubbed it again, a little lower this time.

Oscar set down his fork and again scratched himself, but now he was scratching his forehead.

What had that magician given me, anyway? I wondered. Had he meant the balloon to do this? Then I realized that of course he had meant it! And he had left it up to me, the one kid who wasn't invited to the party, to do with it as I wished.

I looked over. The cake eating was finished, and now everyone lined up in front of Oscar's chair, waiting to give him their presents. I had a fair idea how he might react to his presents. It might be time that Oscar the kitten-kicker was taught a lesson. So I got the balloon all ready and settled back into my chair.

The first party guest in line was Missy Johnson. Oscar snatched the gift from her hands without even reading the card. "I picked it out myself," she said nervously. "I hope you like it . . ."

Oscar's chubby fingers tore into the box, and in another instant he had uncovered a red shirt. Missy must have noticed Oscar's true favorite color as well, I thought.

"I hope you don't think I'm going to *wear* this!" Oscar sneered. "This is just about the ugliest shirt that I—"

"No," I said under my breath. *"Bad* Oscar." And I gave the right side of the balloon a mighty flick with one forefinger.

"Ow!" Oscar suddenly shrieked, lifting both hands toward his right ear.

"What's the matter, Oscar?" Missy said, confused.

"I . . . I don't know," he answered, feeling his tender ear. "For a second there it was like a bee just stung me or something."

I could not keep from smiling.

The next kid in line was Stanley Kobowski. He was one of the shortest kids in school and was very shy about it. He held up a brightly wrapped present to the birthday boy.

"Thanks, shrimp," Oscar said mockingly. He held the gift up, just out of Stanley's reach. "Gee, I hope I'll be able to open this now, I'm a little *short* on time. But maybe I'll be able to open it up *shortly.*"

That's when I clapped my hand over the lower part of the balloon—right where a mouth would be.

"Mmmmph," Oscar mumbled, his lips suddenly pressed tightly together. He started to look distressed, so I let go of the balloon.

"Are you okay?" Stanley asked, concern showing on his face.

Oscar panted for a second, running his fingers over his lips. "Of course I'm okay, short stuff—" he started to say, but I stopped him. "Mmmmph!" he concluded. This time he dropped the present and tried to pry his jaws open. I slowly released my hold on the balloon.

I watched Oscar carefully as he opened up Stanley's gift, which was a new baseball. But he seemed hesitant to say anything mean, so I kept my hands off the balloon. Maybe he was actually learning.

The third person in line was Jeff Trujillo. Jeff had kind of a long face and had been given the nickname "Peanut-head." I was all ready for this one.

Oscar took the present and opened the box, revealing a nice digital watch. He started out well enough. "Thanks," he said at first. But then old Oscar couldn't resist adding just one little put-down. "Peanut-head."

"We'll see who the peanut-head is, Oscar," I said in a low voice. And I carefully stretched the balloon from top to bottom. I looked over. Oscar's face actually grew longer and less plump the further I stretched the balloon. Soon his head looked so much like a peanut that Jeff's looked perfectly normal next to his.

I let go, allowing the balloon—and Oscar's face—to return to normal. Oscar held his face in both hands, obviously wondering what had happened. Jeff, who was the only one at the party who saw the rubbery face he'd made, was stunned. "Wow, Oscar, how did you do that? That was even better than that magician's tricks!" he cried.

Oscar only shook his head, falling back into a chair in exhaustion.

The next guest was Peggy Stoker. Peggy had always been just a little on the heavy side. Not that Oscar could talk, but I knew he wouldn't be able to resist a comment. I was right. Immediately after he unwrapped the model car she'd given him, he thanked her, then weakly started to ask her how many pieces of cake she'd had today. So I socked it to him, flattening the top and bottom ends of the balloon so the middle squished out. In a second, Oscar's head was exactly the same shape as a Halloween pumpkin.

By now the other kids were getting kind of scared by Oscar's weird expressions and behavior. As for Oscar himself, I could see by the look on his face that he wouldn't be making any more mean comments for a long, long time.

I should have stopped there, I know. I had probably done everything the magician had intended when he gave me the balloon. But I just couldn't. I was getting carried away by the power I had over Oscar. For one thing, I began to wonder what would happen if I just let go of the balloon string. Would Oscar's silly head go floating off his shoulders? Curious, I leaned over the sidewalk, and let the balloon go up clear to the top of its string, just to test it out. I was a little disappointed to see that Oscar's head stayed right where it was. He did seem to act dizzy, though.

And that gave me another idea. I took the balloon and began winding it around on its string, over and over again, for about a minute. Then—still holding onto the string, of course—I let it go. The balloon twirled and spun.

I looked over at the patio across the way. Hank Melendez had been trying to hand Oscar his present when suddenly Oscar became so dizzy he fell out of his chair. Hank and the rest of the party-goers stood over him, asking him what was wrong. But Oscar couldn't say a thing until the balloon stopped unwinding.

That's when I took the balloon and started slapping the sides. Oscar cried out and put his head in his hands. The kids called for his mother, who came out and looked into her son's eyes.

"I've got a terrible headache, Mom," Oscar whined. And with that, the party was over. The kids filed out, telling Oscar they hoped he felt better soon.

I stopped slapping the balloon. A horrible thought had just hit me: If I accidentally popped the balloon, would Oscar's head explode?

And then the wizard's last words came back to me: *"Don't do anything you will regret."*

I watched Oscar's mom help him to his bedroom, and I decided it was over. I'd taught him some lessons and messed up the party he'd never invited me to. I never really wanted to hurt him. But there wasn't too much difference between what I had been doing and kicking kittens, when you got right down to it.

Now the question was, what should I do with the balloon? I couldn't exactly let it go, and I sure didn't want to keep it. Finally it hit me. I would sneak over and tie it to the railing on Oscar's fence. They could deal with it.

When no one was looking, I made my way across the courtyard.

The curtains on Oscar's bedroom window were closed, but as I passed by I could hear his mother murmuring to her son inside. Her voice must have distracted me as I leaned over to tie the string to the railing. Suddenly I looked up to see that the black balloon was bumping against the patio ceiling! As I watched, terrified, the bottom of the balloon brushed against the hook Oscar's father had used for the piñata! Terrified, I yanked the balloon down and examined it.

A small hole had been torn in the loose rubber.

"Oh no," I breathed. As I watched, helpless, the black balloon puffed out a steady, feeble jet of air. Slowly it shriveled in my hands until it was the size of a crumpled black flower.

Even worse were the screams of the woman and the boy.

Sleep-over at Annette's

I still can't believe we're sleeping here!" Audrey whispered, stopping dead in her tracks just before the front walk. She looked at the house—a modest home with potted flowers on the windowsills. Audrey's hair shone golden in the setting sun, and she twined one finger through it. "I mean, Nettie is *such* a loser."

"It is kinda weird," Eileen agreed, frowning as she switched her sleeping bag to the other arm. "We've never had anything to do with her in our lives and suddenly old Nerdie Nettie goes and invites us to a sleep-over!"

Susie giggled under her breath and strolled ahead up the walk, leading the others as usual. "Come on, you two!" she commanded. "It doesn't matter whose idea it was! This will

75

be educational. You'll see. All we're doing is spending an evening here so we can learn how geeks live their lives."

"Okay, when you put it *that* way," Audrey said, a nasty smile slowly returning to her face. "I guess it will be pretty entertaining at that."

Without further delay all three girls reached forward and knocked on the door.

The door swung open, and a girl their own age stood awkwardly before them. She wore thick glasses and a long polka-dot dress.

"Hi, Nettie," the girls gushed, as if she were their best friend.

"Don't you look great in that spotty dress!" Audrey added with false enthusiasm.

"Thanks," Annette said shyly. She did not make eye contact with any of them. "Come on in . . . and meet my parents." Annette stiffly turned around. When they were sure she wasn't looking, the three girls rolled their eyes at each other, then followed their hostess inside.

Behind the door was a small living room filled with bookcases and old chairs and end tables. Two middle-aged adults rose from a huge orange sofa.

"These are my parents," Annette said in a choked voice. "Mom and Dad, this is Audrey, Eileen, and Susie."

Annette's father was tall and handsome, and he bowed and took off an old-fashioned felt hat. "It's wonderful to meet you," he said politely. "We've heard so much about you!"

Annette's mom, also good-looking, glided from one girl to another, formally shaking their hands. Two gold bracelets jingled on one of her forearms with a *ching-ching* sound.

"We're so glad you could come to Annette's little party," she said.

"Oh," Susie said, putting her hand on her chest dramatically, "we wouldn't have missed it for the world."

Annette's dad replaced his hat and gestured toward the dining table, on which sat chilled soda bottles and glasses. Steam curled from the white cardboard of a pair of pizza boxes. "Here's dinner," he said. "Hope you like pizza!"

The woman moved to stand next to her husband. "Well, good night. We'll let you kids enjoy yourselves," she said with a smile.

"Annette, don't forget to lock up at the end of the evening!" her dad said. Annette nodded. Then the man turned to the girls again. "And thank you *so much* for accepting our daughter's invitation." He tipped his hat once more, his wife bowed, and both of them exited through the tall hall doors, shutting them behind them.

For several minutes after their departure there was silence in the room. Annette stood by the dining table, her arms crossed over her chest, lips trembling slightly. The girls stood around her like wolves circling a lamb. Finally, after she was sure the adults were gone, Susie uttered a little chuckle. "So those are the people who adopted you, huh?" she hissed. "Now, be honest with us, Nettie. How long did it take you to teach them to greet guests?"

"What do you mean?" Annette responded, her face blank.

"Oh, you know," Eileen joined in. She snatched a small pillow off the orange sofa and placed it on her head like a hat. "It was so *nice* of you to come!" she said in a whiny, mocking tone, lifting the pillow as if she were tipping the hat. "Oh, I'm so *pleased* to meet you!"

Audrey smirked at her two friends. "Well, at least we learned something interesting. Nettie's parents are just as geeky as *she* is!"

Annette turned to the table as her three guests dissolved into helpless laughter. "Should we . . . have some pizza before it gets cold?" she asked in a desperate attempt to change the subject.

Susie strutted over and flung open the lids on the boxes. "What is this? Pineapple?" She wrinkled her nose in distaste. "Who in their right mind would want to eat *that* on their pizza?"

Annette shook her head. "I-I'm sorry," she said. "We just thought . . ."

"Well, you just should have asked us first, shouldn't you have?" Susie scolded.

Eileen moved to stand over the boxes, where she plucked pieces of fruit off the pizza, flinging them carelessly onto the table. When she was done, the three friends all took slices of pizza from the box.

"We only eat *cheese* pizza," Susie mumbled through a full mouth. "Remember that for next time!"

Sighing, Annette sat down on a chair, watching while the three girls wolfed down the pizza. When they finished, she cleared her throat and brought out a box that had been sitting under her chair. "Would you . . . all like to play some games now?" she asked quietly. "We have Chinese checkers, chess, and all kinds of card games."

"I don't think so," Susie snapped back. "I think what we'd mainly like to do is just talk, wouldn't we, girls?" She smiled at the others, who grinned back and pulled their chairs up around Annette.

"Yeah," agreed Audrey. "Let's just get to know each other better."

And so, for the next couple of hours, Annette stayed rooted to her chair, her face cast down, while the other girls took turns insulting her, each one crueler than the last.

"Those are real cool games you have there, Nettie. Checkers, chess, and cards—how *original*."

"So, where *did* you get that awful dress, anyway?"

"Who decorated this awful house? Pigs from the local barnyard?"

"Do you ever wonder how come no one likes to sit next to you at school?"

Annette gave one-word answers to their questions. Sometimes she shrugged. And sometimes she just tried to ignore them. All the while she cast frequent glances at the mantel clock. When it was finally midnight she slowly rose from her chair with a tired but relieved expression on her face.

"Hey, I've got one more question," Susie said. "Your parents said they'd heard a lot about us. Just what kind of stuff did you tell them, anyway?"

"Did you make up a bunch of lies about the things we all do together and the places we go?" Eileen prompted.

"I'll bet you said what great friends we were, right?" Audrey added, playing with her hair again. "You probably went on and on about how cool and considerate we are, and how much you like us, and how much our friendship means to you."

Annette cleared her throat and sighed. "Actually, I told them you're the meanest, most gossipy kids in the school, and that you're incredibly stuck on yourselves," she said, pushing her glasses back up on her nose with one thumb. "And I made it pretty clear that I don't like any of you. But then, that's exactly why I invited the three of you over here."

Utter silence filled the room. The trio looked from one to the other with wide, shocked eyes. Susie, as usual, was the first one to recover. "That doesn't make any sense!" she protested. "Why would you ask us to spend the night if you couldn't stand us?"

"Believe me, it was only because my parents asked me to," Annette said with a sigh. She looked at her watch. "Time to lock up," she murmured, and she went around securely locking each door in the room.

"They were probably worried because you never bring any friends home, right?" sneered Audrey.

"Did they really think this would work?" Eileen said. "Did your parents really believe they could *buy* you our friendship with some pizza and an invitation to stay in your dump of a house?"

Annette, who was finished with the locks, faced them squarely. "Not even close," she said wistfully, looking out the window as a stray moonbeam lit her face. "It really didn't have anything to do with me. My parents were just hungry, that's all."

"Hungry?" said Susie. She made a face to the others and twirled one finger next to her temple. "That's a pretty weird comment. Even for *you*, Nerdy Nettie. What in the world are you babbling about?"

Audrey, who had wandered off to the side of the room, craned her head this way and that as she studied one of the doors. "Hey!" she finally said, tugging on the knob. The sarcasm was gone, and her voice sounded alarmed. "Why are these doors all locked? Annette, what's going on? Why did you shut the doors?"

"So you can't get out," Annette answered calmly. And with that, she turned around and opened the hall doors.

The wolflike creatures on the other side stood there on hind legs, glowering at the girls with sharp, yellow eyes. One of them wore an old-fashioned felt hat. The animal-thing was so tall that the hat almost brushed the ceiling. The other had two gold bracelets encircling a hairy forepaw. The bracelets rang together with a *ching-ching* as both creatures dropped to all fours.

"Sorry. I left out one little detail when I told you I was adopted," Annette said with a sly grin. "I was adopted by werewolves!"

With ferocious, mad-dog growls, Annette's parents bounded into the room after the screaming girls.

Christmas at Mountain Hollow

imothy's father drove the car carefully over the icy road. From underneath the vehicle came the sound of the snow chains, rhythmically bumping metal with each turn of the tire. Outside, the trees, ground, and boulders were all covered in a fluffy blanket of snow.

"Timothy, can you believe we're actually going to have our first white Christmas?" six-year-old Nicole said happily.

"I know. It's going to be pretty cool," Timothy answered. He smiled, looking over at his sister, who had her face pressed against the glass, staring out in wonder at the wintry scene. He was looking forward to their holiday up in the mountains, too. But he had also been just the tiniest bit afraid as well.

He looked out the window just in time to see a city limits sign with icicles dripping from its bottom edge. MOUNTAIN HOLLOW, POPULATION 750. Timothy shuddered at the sight. Was it possible that what he had heard about this place was true?

"Almost there," their father said from the front seat.

Their mother turned around and gave them the thumbs-up sign. "I can hardly wait!" she said excitedly.

"Me neither!" squeaked Nicole.

Timothy smiled at them and nodded. He wished he felt the family's enthusiasm for this particular vacation. From under the car, the snow chains continued to bump, sounding to Timothy like a cold heart beating in the forest.

They pulled off the main road and reached the isolated rental cabin a few minutes later. It was a small, single-level structure made of pine that still had the bark attached. This gave it an old-fashioned look. Icicles hung from the eaves, and a layer of snow covered the roof like frosting on a cake.

"We're here!" Timothy's father announced, pulling the car into the driveway. No sooner had he turned off the engine than the entire family flung open their doors, opened the front gate, and stamped a path through the snow to the front porch.

Inside, the cabin was very inviting. Warm wood covered nearly every surface. A huge rock fireplace stood in the living room, and soon Timothy's father had a blazing fire going. After they all had unpacked their suitcases, the family relaxed on the big sofa before the crackling flames.

"Didja notice?" Nicole said, pointing at the wide wooden mantel. "It's perfect for hanging our stockings! Can we put 'em up now, please?"

Her father glanced at his watch. "It's a little late now, honey," he said.

Her mother looked at her and winked. "Christmas is the day after tomorrow," she said. "In the morning we'll all start decorating. But for tonight I think it's time to test those electric blankets in our rooms, don't you?"

Everyone nodded sleepily and trudged off to bed. Nicole, in the same room as Timothy, chattered to him about Christmas for a few minutes. Then she fell silent, and soon Timothy heard the even sound of her breathing as she slept. Timothy snuggled into his own sheets and slowly dropped off to sleep.

It was still dark when he awoke. He had distinctly heard the sound of something heavily walking through the snow outside. Timothy got out of bed and crept to the window, the crunching sound still vibrating in his ears. *Could it be?* he thought in fear. When he swept the drapes aside, it was hard to make anything out, since the full moon was shining directly in the glass. When his eyes adjusted, he thought he saw an odd white figure moving off behind the pine trees not one hundred feet away, but it disappeared so suddenly, Timothy couldn't really be sure.

He waited some time, watching the dark forest, but nothing else happened. Finally, Timothy grew chilled from standing at the icy window, and he jumped back into bed. He shivered there for a long time, both from cold and fear.

．．．．．．．．．．．

The next time Timothy awoke, it was from the pressure of a hand on his shoulder. His eyes flew open, and it was all he

could do to keep from screaming. But it was just his father, sitting on the mattress, the morning sun coloring the curtains gold behind him. "Sorry. I didn't mean to startle you," he whispered. "It's Christmas Eve morning, and I thought we could surprise your mom and sister by picking out our tree before they wake up!"

"Okay, Dad. Sounds good," Timothy whispered back, feeling weak. He glanced over at Nicole, who still lay peacefully sleeping.

"Dress warmly. I'll wait for you in the living room," his father said, and he left so Timothy could get ready.

Outside it was very cold. Timothy could see his breath like a cloud before his face. His father held a big ax in one mittened hand and gestured toward the forest with the other. "Now, let's each look around for the perfect tree. When you see a good one, call out to me, and if we agree, we'll cut it down, okay?"

Timothy looked around, blinking. "You mean we're going to split up?" he asked, alarmed.

"Sure! That way we can look at more trees," his father said cheerfully. "But don't go too far from the cabin!" And with that, he walked off, swinging his ax, and was soon swallowed up by the forest.

Timothy looked about. At least the sky was blue and the sun was bright. *I'll surely be safe in broad daylight, won't I?* he thought uncertainly, trying to convince himself. Then he nervously walked off into the trees.

After a while he saw several fir trees that were very pretty, but they were either too short or too tall. *Maybe the perfect one will be right around the next corner,* he thought, wondering if his father was having the same kind of luck.

But then Timothy made the mistake of looking down. A set of long, clawlike footprints was etched into the icy surface of the snow at his feet, and he realized he had wandered to the same section of the forest where he'd seen the white shape the night before! He stared down at the prints, speechless with fear.

Suddenly a shout rose from the pines over to the left. "Timothy! Come over this way!" his father yelled. "I've got a great tree here."

Without thinking, Timothy bolted through the trees toward where he'd heard his father's voice. After a few feet the ground became rough, and he had to climb over several rocks before entering the forest again. Every time he brushed past a tree, Timothy braced himself, expecting to run up against whatever it was that had made those footprints. But finally he broke through into a little clearing where his father was proudly pointing at a tree. "Look, here's the one I—" his father began.

"Dad! We have to get out of here!" Timothy interrupted, looking over his shoulder. "We're not alone in this forest!"

His father's smile faded from his face. "What do you mean, *not alone?*"

"I mean, kids from school warned me that some kind of *snowbeast* lives in Mountain Hollow," Timothy said breathlessly. "Last night I think I saw it, and just now I found its footprints!"

His father sighed. "Look, I'll make a deal with you. Let's cut down this tree first, then we'll check out those footprints, all right?"

Timothy agreed, and he waited, nervously looking around, while his dad chopped down the fir tree. Then the two of them carried it, his father holding the big stump and Timothy the smaller end.

"I think the prints are over this way," Timothy said as he tried to retrace his steps, leading back through the forest the way he'd come. But at the boulders he couldn't even find his *own* footprints. At last he had to shrug. "I can't remember where I saw the prints," he admitted. "But they were there."

His father paused and looked Timothy in the eye. "Look, I believe you when you say you saw something that scared you," he said. "And I want you to come to me or your mom if you see anything else. But in the meantime, let's not mention this to your sister, okay? We don't want anything to ruin her Christmas!"

Timothy nodded, and the two dragged their prize tree back to the cabin.

....

The rest of the day was spent decorating the tree and the cabin. Nicole and her mom were in charge of the tree, and they hung every one of the family ornaments, in addition to homemade popcorn strings and lights. Meanwhile, Timothy and his dad strung lights inside and outside the cabin and hung up a wreath. They took a break for lunch and later ate a big turkey dinner. Then they sang carols, while Timothy and Nicole hung up their stockings on nails that their dad drove into the mantelpiece.

It was a fun day. But even so, the thought of the snowbeast was there in the back of Timothy's mind, taunting him throughout the evening. He felt he had to do something to protect his family. Earlier he'd noticed that the long string of sleigh bells his family usually put up on their front door at home was still lying at the bottom of one of the boxes of Christmas decorations. Just before bedtime, while Nicole was setting out milk and cookies for Santa, he retrieved the sleigh bells. Then he snuck out into the dark, snow-filled yard and hung them on the front gate. The gate provided the only way into the yard, and Timothy figured that now they would at least have some kind of warning if an unexpected visitor came calling in the night.

It wasn't much, but he felt better doing something rather than nothing at all. Timothy had a feeling his family was about to experience a Christmas Eve unlike any other.

···········

Late that night Timothy felt little fingers shaking him awake. It was Nicole, a look of wonder stamped on her features. "Listen, Timothy!" she whispered. "Do you hear it?"

Timothy felt his eyes widening as he heard a tinkling sound from somewhere outside. All of a sudden he realized what it was. "S-s-sleighbells!" he stuttered.

"Of course, silly," Nicole whispered. "Isn't it *wonderful?* Santa must be here!"

Timothy stared at her for a second, then nodded dumbly. "Well . . . y-y-yes," he said, not wanting to upset her. *"That must be who it is . . ."* Timothy chewed on his lower lip, racking his brain for a plan.

Suddenly his sister crept toward the window. "Maybe we can see him from here," she whispered in an awestruck tone, reaching for the curtains.

"No!" Timothy shouted. He threw himself out of bed and darted in front of Nicole to block her view. The last thing they needed was for her to start crying or yelling right now. Nicole stared at him with a hurt expression. "Uh . . . Santa might be shy about someone . . . seeing him," he explained haltingly.

In spite of his words, Timothy could not resist pulling the curtains aside and sneaking a peek of his own out the glass.

The gate stood ajar, just as he feared. Timothy scanned the rest of the yard, and his jaw dropped open. *Walking across the sidewalk toward the house was a hairy white creature nearly eight feet tall.* Evidently, it had just made a kill before entering their yard, for it carried the body of a deer on its broad shoulders. It twisted its shaggy head to take a bite of its prize, its sharp teeth tearing the raw meat as if it were paper.

Stunned, Timothy looked back into the room. The streaming moonlight threw the shadow of the deer's antlered head onto the wall, and Nicole was pointing at it in glee. "I can see the shadow of a reindeer, right there, Tim!" she said. Then she frowned at Timothy. "How come *you* get to look at Santa and I don't?" she asked in a snippy tone.

Timothy glanced at the yard once more, just in time to see the beast casually toss the buck off into the snow. It turned to stare up at the cabin with narrow, scowling eyes and smacked its black lips. Then, without warning, it crouched and leaped onto the outside wall, scaling the roof in a few easy motions.

Timothy looked back, giving Nicole his most stern expression. "Nicole, you *have* to stay here in the room for a minute!" He spoke quickly, his words tumbling over one another. "I've got to talk to Mom and Dad, okay?"

She nodded, but it was plain by her expression that she was both confused and angry over her brother's orders.

Easing their bedroom door closed behind him, Timothy raced down the hall into his parents' room. "Mom! Dad!" he said urgently. "You've got to get up!"

Moaning, his parents rolled over in their bed. "What's wrong, son?" his dad asked, blinking in the gloom. He reached for a bedside light, but Timothy put his hand out to stop him.

"You know that thing I told you about this morning?" he said breathlessly. "Well, it's *here*. I just saw it climb onto the roof! I think it's trying to find a way in!"

As if to punctuate his sentence, an abrupt scraping noise grated from above their heads. His parents sat up in their bed, suddenly wide awake. Then they all heard a door swing open, and footsteps pounding down the hall in their direction. Nicole's face appeared at the open doorway. "Did you all hear that?" she said blissfully. "It must be Santa on the roof!"

In the dim moonlight creeping in through cracks in the curtains, Timothy saw his parents exchange a look. "What should we do?" his mother whispered.

Her husband shrugged. "We may have to leave," he said solemnly. "Timothy, how big was this thing you saw?"

"Its head would touch the ceiling!" Timothy told them.

Another scraping issued from above, louder this time. Nicole ran out of the room.

"Nicole!" yelled her mom.

For a few seconds there was no answer. Then Nicole's voice called from the living room, "Hurry, everybody! I think he's coming down the chimney now!"

Moving as one person, Timothy and his parents rushed out the door and into the front room. A clattering sound issued from the chimney. To Timothy's horror, his sister knelt on the hearth with her head gazing up into the fireplace. "Santa," she cooed. "You're not really too shy to be seen, are you?"

"Nicole, come here this *instant!*" their mother yelled.

The little girl backed up and took a step toward them. The scrambling sounds intensified, followed by a clattering. Several bricks rained down into the fireplace, right on the spot where Nicole had been perched. She stared down at the damage and looked up at her family with a smirk. "I think Santa's having trouble getting down the chimney!" she giggled. "Maybe we should just open the front door and let him in!"

Her father grabbed her hand, hustled her into the hall, and motioned for his wife and son to follow. There was a terrified look in his eye that Timothy had never seen before. "Listen. I want you three to wait down the hall, out of sight of the living room. I'm just going in our bedroom for the car keys, okay?"

Behind him, the crashing noises grew louder. More bricks came spilling into the living room. "But Dad," Nicole said, clearly puzzled.

"Now!" the father ordered, and their mom hustled the kids to the end of the hall while he darted into the bedroom.

There was a final tremendous crash from the living room, then everything fell strangely silent. Their father reappeared after a second, clutching the keys in one hand. "What happened?" he asked, his voice a whisper.

"Maybe he gave up," his wife whispered hopefully.

Or maybe, Timothy thought, *he got inside.*

"I hope you're right," the man said to his wife. "Because this hall is a dead end—we have to pass the living room to get out the front door to get to the car!"

Everyone listened for a few seconds, but the house was silent.

"I don't understand," Nicole said in a low voice. "Why are we leaving? Where are we going?"

Nicole's mother reached over and hugged her. "We'll explain everything later," she said.

From the next room came the sound of breaking glass. "Okay, on the count of three," the children's father said, his voice hoarse. "We're going to make a run for it. Hold hands and follow me. One . . . two . . . THREE!"

The entire family bolted down the hall past the living room. Timothy stopped and stared in at the wreckage of the fireplace, looking anxiously among the scattered bricks for signs of the snowbeast. "Look! Look at the table! Santa ate his milk and cookies!" Nicole suddenly cried.

Timothy noticed a few shards of porcelain lying on the table's surface.

"Shhh!" their mother warned. Their father opened the front door and ushered everyone out, but it was already too late. Timothy glanced back and saw a huge, hairy head peek around the corner from the kitchen. "Run!" he screamed.

The four of them took off, snow kicking up in clots from the slippers on their feet. Timothy's father had unlocked the car and already had the key in the ignition before the others had reached it. The engine made a grinding noise. *Was it too cold to start?* Timothy wondered frantically. He looked behind him, just as the snowbeast flew out the front door.

94

Timothy's mother picked Nicole up and leaped into the backseat. Meanwhile his father turned the key again, and this time the engine caught.

Timothy opened the passenger door and started to get in, but something seemed to be holding him back. He looked down. His bathrobe pocket was twisted around the door handle, keeping him in place like a dog on a leash. Timothy struggled, thrashing back and forth in an effort to free himself.

Heavy footsteps crunched on the snow after him.

"Hurry, Timothy!" his dad yelled. He kept the car idling, waiting for his son to get in. Suddenly the night seemed to grow darker. Timothy knew the beast was right next to him, blocking the moonlight with its huge body. Frantic at the thought, Timothy threw himself violently to one side, and the pocket of the bathrobe ripped off entirely. He was free!

"Go, Dad!" he yelled as he leaped into the front passenger seat. His father hit the gas, and the car began to lurch away.

But Timothy could not shut his door. The snowbeast held on to it with one powerful hand, and was running alongside the car, its snarling face lunging through the door opening at Timothy. It opened its fanged mouth, preparing to bite him.

His mother screamed from the backseat. Nicole, sheltered from the awful sight by her mother's arms, yelled, "Let me go! What's happening?"

The car gained speed, but the beast kept pace with the car, still holding the door open. Its drooling mouth moved in toward Timothy. His father, careful not to slow down the car, suddenly lunged for the door handle and tugged the door out of the beast's grasp. The door glanced off the creature's snapping jaws, pinching its face as it closed. Then Timothy's dad jammed the gas pedal to the floor. Pinwheels of snow flew from the tires, and the snow chains began slapping the underside of the car.

Timothy looked behind them. The creature was stunned by the impact from the door. It simply stood in place for a few seconds, fingering its cheek where a patch of white hair had been ripped away. It made a halfhearted attempt to follow the car, then finally gave up.

"All right, Dad!" Timothy yelled. "We did it!"

············

Later the family settled in to spend Christmas Eve in a hotel room. Timothy's father came over and sat on the edge of his mattress and offered him a tired smile. "Thanks for warning us about that thing," he whispered. "You really saved us all."

"Yes, Timothy," his mom added. "You were very brave."

Timothy nodded at them. "Thanks for listening to me," he said. He glanced around at the small, undecorated hotel room. Christmas hadn't turned out the way any of them had planned, but they were all safe, and right now Timothy thought that was the only thing he would have asked for.

He looked over at his little sister in the next bed, but Nicole was already asleep. Clutched between her fingers was a swatch of white fur she'd found inside the car, torn from the snowbeast when the door closed on its face.

She thought she'd found a piece of Santa Claus's beard, and no one in the family could talk her into giving it up.